THIS IS BASEBALL

by Margaret Blackstone
pictures by John O'Brien

SQUARE FISH ◆ Henry Holt and Company ◆ New York

For my father, Henry
my son, Dash
my husband, Tom
and my brothers, Pete and Neil
all great boys of summer
and for my friend, Elissa
one of the great girls of all seasons
—M.B.

For Tessie,
the first in my lineup
—J.O'B.

SQUARE
FISH

An Imprint of Macmillan
175 Fifth Avenue, New York, NY 10010
mackids.com

Library of Congress Cataloging-in-Publication Data
Blackstone, Margaret / This is baseball / by Margaret Blackstone; pictures by John O'Brien.
Summary: A simple introduction to the game of baseball, covering its equipment, players, and basic plays.
The illustrations show the game in progress.   I. Baseball—Juvenile literature. (I. Baseball)
I. O'Brien, John, ill.   II. Title. GV867.5.B57 1993   796.357—dc20   92-22921   ISBN 978-0-8050-5169-8

Originally published in the United States by Henry Holt and Company
First Square Fish Edition: 2013
Square Fish logo designed by Filomena Tuosto
20   19

AR: 1.1

THIS IS BASEBALL

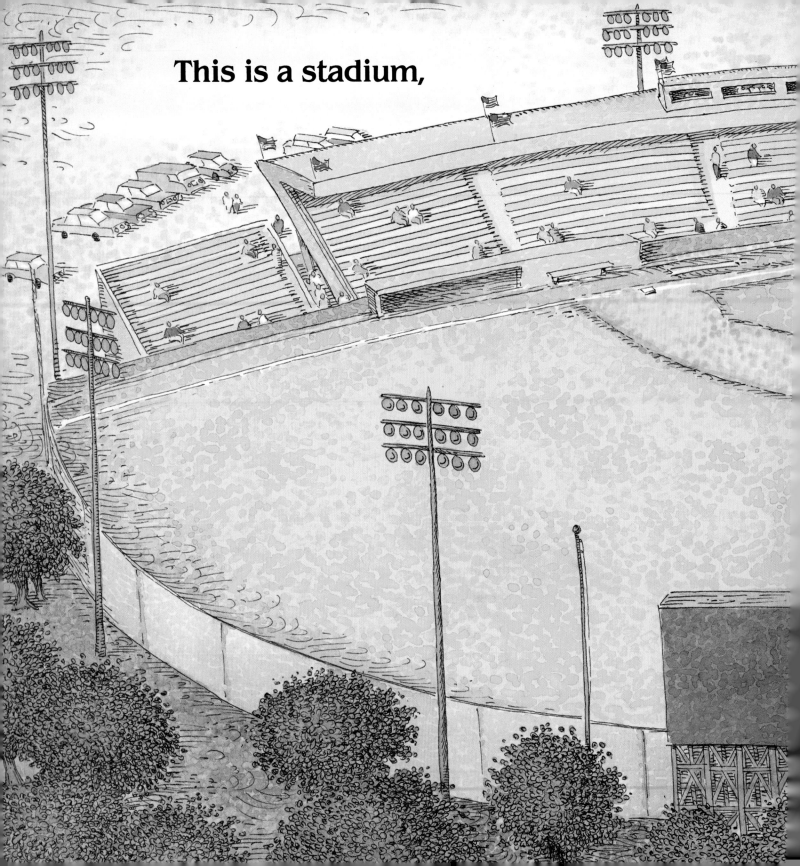

This is a stadium,

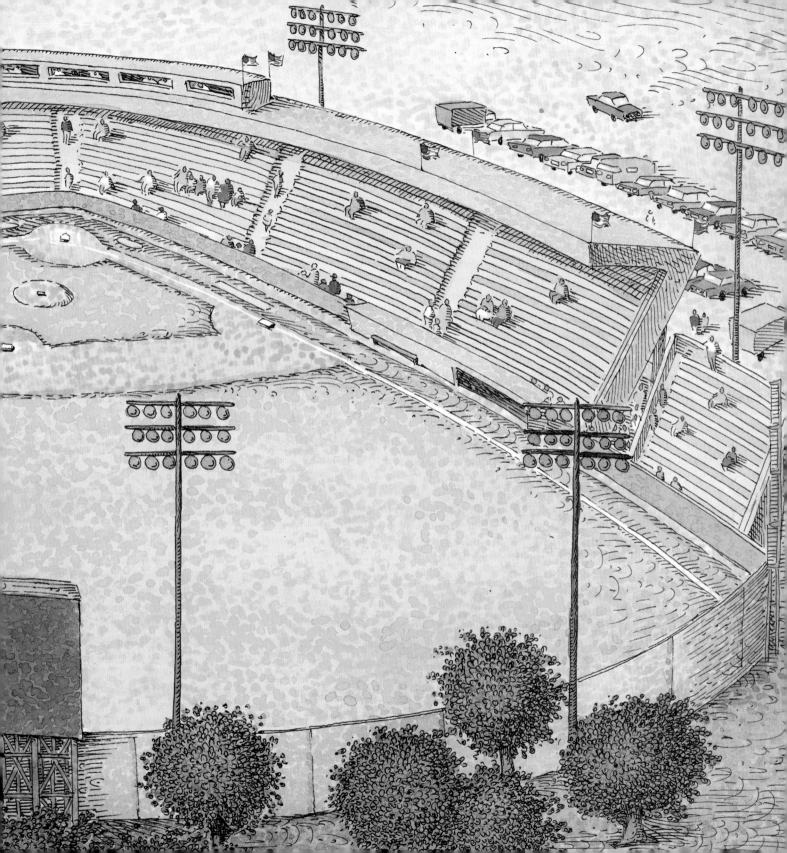

and this is a baseball diamond.

This is one team,

and this is the other.

These are the fans.

This is a ball,

and this is a bat.

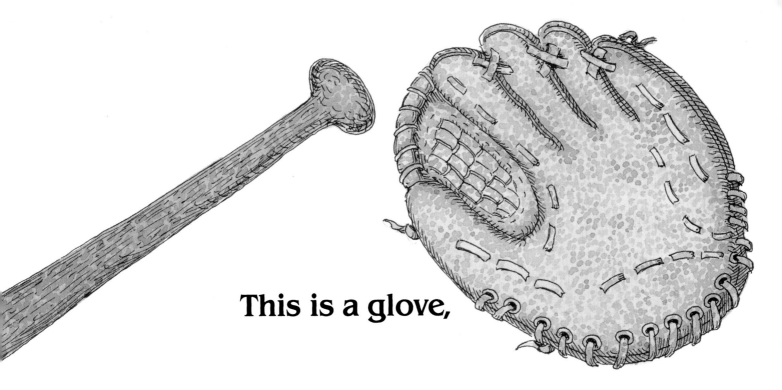

This is a glove,

and this is a cap.

This is a player.

And these are the umpires who call the game.

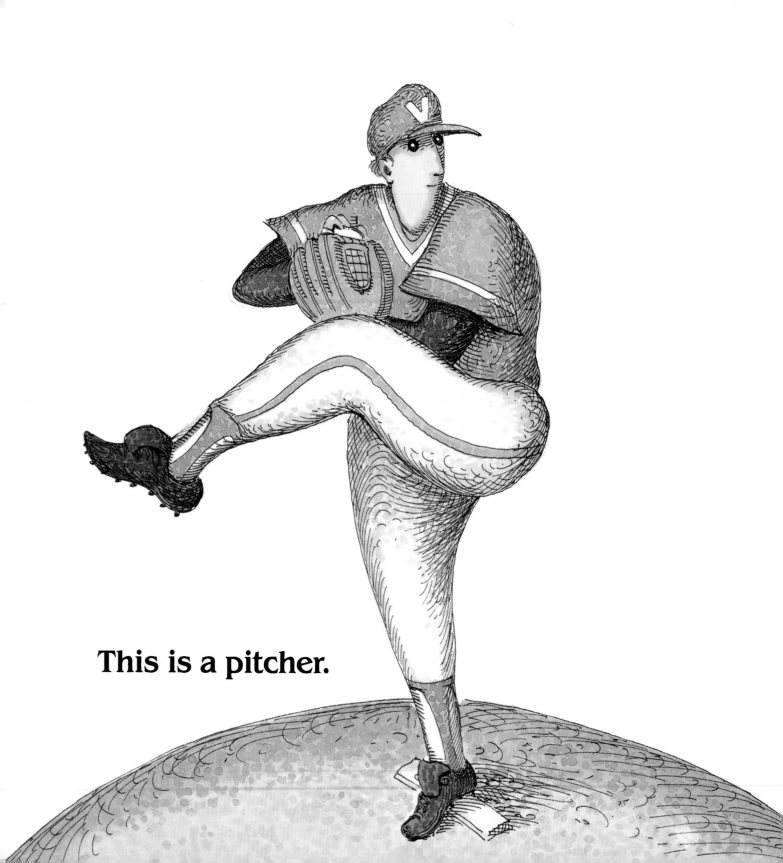

This is a pitcher.

This is a catcher.

This is the infield.

STRIKE
BALL 3
20
AT BAT
1 2 3 4 5 6
VISITORS 0 0 0 2 0 1
HOME 0 1 0 0 1 0
31

This is the outfield.

This is a pitch.

And this is a hit!

This is a high fly ball to deep left field...

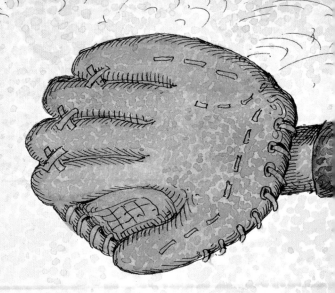

and this is a
HOME RUN!

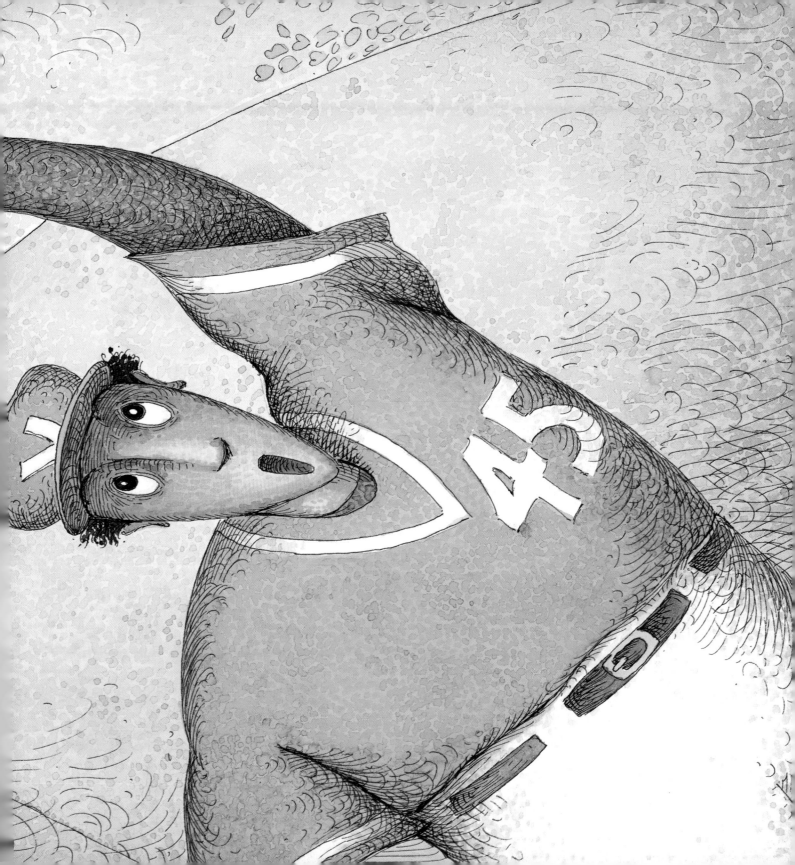

This team has won,

and this team has lost.

Tomorrow there will be another game.